a DAYS OF SPANIARD story
from

The Spaniard

With lessons and cliffhangers
all along the way

PARENTS | GUARDIANS | TEACHERS
Please consider reading & discussing this book with your child, student or group over 30 days.
Turn the page to see the reason.

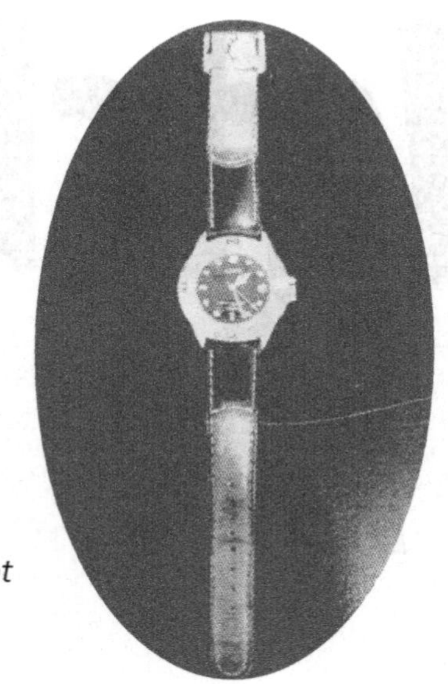

The actual watch from the 1990s that inspired this story

ISBN 9798854436359

This is a work of fiction based on the life and work of Charlie "THE SPANIARD" Brenneman and blends fact with fiction. Names, characters, places and incidents are products of imagination or are used fictitiously. The Creative Lead for the DAYS OF SPANIARD series is Keith "DREAD" Eldred, who drafts the stories and refines them with THE SPANIARD.

KIDS ARE WORTH TAKING TIME

This book is designed for
parents, guardians and teachers
to share with young people
in short sessions across 30 days.

Of course, instead you can
read the book straight through.

But please consider going slow
and giving your young audience
something special to look back on—
a time when a caring adult
wanted to talk with them
over and over and over.

In the end, DAYS OF SPANIARD
is not about THE SPANIARD.
It's about the days.

See the end of this book for a
TEACHING GUIDE WITH QUESTIONS
to help meet instructional standards,
teach students life skills,
and measure understanding

Hey, let's dive into a story meant to be told over 30 days!

In the pages of this book, the story is on the RIGHT and lessons that go along are on the LEFT. Enjoy and learn!

Thanks!

- Spaniard

Dedicated to every kid
who's been picked on, bullied,
targeted or made to feel bad.

It's never easy, and it's never right. But trust me when I say that you CAN get through it, and that there are people who care. Let this book and these words be your reminder that you're never alone.

Listening is a great way to help others. Think of those times when you need to tell what's on your mind to someone you can trust. Be the person who listens without judging and who helps protect the privacy of others.

1

I have the great joy of getting to visit schools across the country to speak at assemblies.

The school leaders also sometimes arrange for me to go to lunch periods to spend time with students.

Kids often come up to me and tell me things that they say they've never told anyone—about how they're hurting and what they're facing.

I want to tell you about one girl I talked with who I'll call Nicki.

It was due to a problem with bullying.

Bullying is like dark clouds entering a bright sky. At its best, school is a safe and friendly place for learning. Everyone receives respect. Adults help and support students. But bullying changes everything. It ruins school days and sometimes lives.

2

At assemblies, one thing I talk about is being targeted at school when I was young. You'll hear more about that later.

I can see the information landing with students as well as teachers, because bullying is far too common.

At the school that Nicki attended, I was approached by a teacher who I'll call Señora Cruz.

She said, "I'd like to follow up with you on what you said about bullying."

When adults look back on their early years at those who helped them and cared for them, many think of teachers. Not only because of classroom instruction but because those teachers enjoyed them, watched out for them and helped them grow as people.

3

Señora Cruz told me about Nicki.

"I think it would be good for you to talk to her, with me on hand. Would you have a few minutes to meet with us?"

I said I could, after the lunch periods.

I asked Señora Cruz to briefly tell me more about what she was thinking, and more about Nicki.

Take it from someone who's been there: Most professional fighters are driven by the challenge more than the money they might make. It's not about violence from anger. It's a huge test of preparation and focus that happens within rules. Fighters do get scared—often very, very scared. We just refuse to give in to our fears. Many of us just want the thrill and satisfaction of pushing our limits.

Señora Cruz had seen Nicki perk up at particular times during my talk. The first time was during the video showing highlights of my professional fighting career.

She said that Nicki listened intently when I talked about progressing from grade school wrestling to mixed martial arts as an amateur and pro and finally to the UFC.

Kids are often amazed to learn that, years before my time in the Octagon, I was as small and scared as any of them—and that, just like everyone, I have never stopped having various kinds of fear.

Now back to another time during my talk when Nicki perked up.

Image by Clker-Free-Vector-Images from Pixabay

Crabs give a picture of attacking someone else's special effort. When a bucket is full of crabs, and one starts to climb out, other crabs pull it back. It's as if they're saying, "If I can't have it, you can't either." Bullying is often driven by jealousy and spite. Don't be that way. Celebrate the wins of others and learn from them. Lift each other up.

5

"You talked about being cyber-bullied," Señora Cruz mentioned.

Yes, I had described haters who hid behind screen names to slam my fighting, and how online trolls bash anyone doing anything unusual—or any target they choose. I told how, before I learned to ignore this stuff, it felt like punches to my gut.

Señora Cruz said that she was watching Nicki closely at that point.

She told me more about what was going on with Nicki.

It was sad to hear about this bullying, because it was like what I'd seen many times.

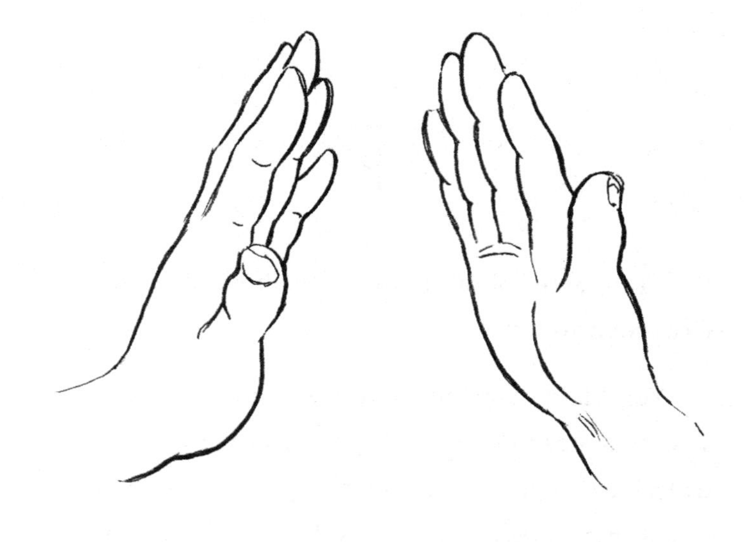

It's called The Golden Rule: **Treat others the way you would like to be treated.** *It's an easy test of how to behave toward someone else. Whatever you're doing or thinking about doing, ask yourself, "Would I want someone to do this to me?" If the answer is no, don't do it. If the answer is yes, do it!*

Señora Cruz told me about the bullying that she had witnessed.

There was lying.

There was name-calling.

There were small cruelties like tripping.

There was pushing and stepping on shoes.

Señora Cruz's description reminded me of things I had experienced—you'll hear more about that later.

I said that I would be glad to speak to Nicki and hoped that I could help.

Female wrestling and fighting have come a long way in recent years. More and more girls and women are dedicating their lives to these sports. My opinion is that it's about dedication and respect. Anyone and everyone has the ability to give their all. And wrestling, in particular, has probably been the greatest teacher in my life. I welcome every boy, girl, man and woman to the #1 sport on Earth!

I'll add this, though, because I know what some of you are thinking: Learning any combat sport is NEVER for the purpose of being a bully, nor specifically for using it on bullies.

7

I had a great time in the lunch periods, then Señora Cruz brought me to a classroom.

Then Señora Cruz brought in Nicki.

I started by chatting and answering some extra questions that Nicki had about fighting.

She was especially curious what I thought about females and fighting, and I told her. I could see her keen interest, and I thought back to being a student, having to stay ready to defend myself and wanting to be able to.

Señora Cruz found an opening to bring us all to the reason we were there.

As I try to help others, I use stories as much as possible. Learning through stories is born into all humans, because understanding people and situations helped our oldest ancestors survive, and sharing those understandings helped others survive. So it's built into all of us to listen to stories like our lives depend on them.

Señora Cruz said to Nicki, "I told The Spaniard that we've been talking about bullying in class and trying to prevent it."

Nicki looked uncomfortable, even miserable.

I said, "Nicki, can I tell you a story about being targeted by a bully when I was your age?"

She nodded yes.

Much of life is about choices. If you skip a party to study for a test, and it's completely up to you, that's a choice. Another person might choose the party because they feel they've studied enough. You might be questioned or even picked on for a choice you make. It can get complicated! Ask caring adults to help you understand making choices.

This story is from my middle school years, long before I was called The Spaniard. Everyone just called me Charlie.

In school, my life was my family, studying, wrestling and hanging out with friends.

Plus avoiding bullies. I would sometimes get picked on for being a goody-goody who didn't go to wild parties or get mixed up in trouble.

You might be surprised at how I thought back then about bullies.

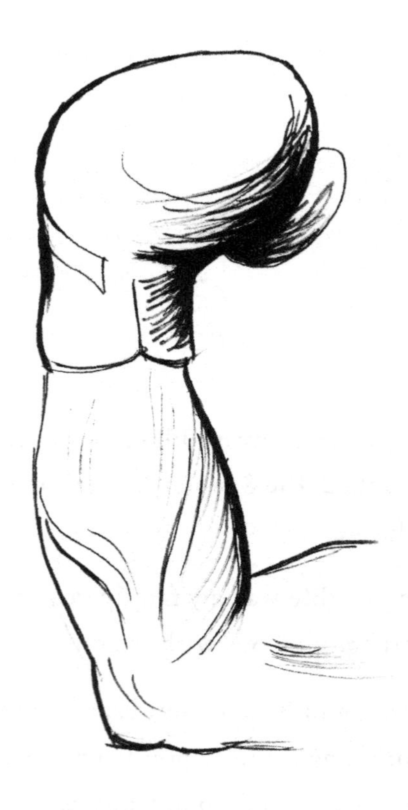

The character Rocky Balboa is a role model as a fighter because of his big heart. That's also why in the first Rocky movie he FAILS at being a bully. He's hired to chase down people and collect money that they owe, but he's too kind to them to do a good job. So Rocky is even a role model for bullies!

Even though I had already been wrestling for years and was strong and in great shape, I was terrified of finding myself in a fight and getting into trouble.

At the same time, my hero was Rocky Balboa from the *Rocky* movies, so I loved the idea of being a fighter even when I was afraid.

I just tried to keep my head down and play it safe.

But there came a time when I couldn't avoid conflict.

What is your treasure? The most precious thing you have? Why? That is great to think about and talk about with a friend. It might be a photo, a ring, a phone, a car—almost anything. But here is something else to think and talk about: Does anything you own … own you? Does it drain your energy or your money or in some other way hold you prisoner? Watch out! That does happen.

11

At this particular time, I got excited about a style of watch that had become popular. I went on and on about it to my friends, but one particular bully overheard me (call him Smash), and used the information to needle me.

"That's too much watch for a runt like you," he jeered. That kind of thing.

So this is what I did about it.

Image by prettysleepy1 from Pixabay

To some of you, an indoor shopping mall might seem like a piece of history, because they have become less popular. In the U.S., the first modern-type shopping mall opened in 1955, and new malls were built every year for about 50 years straight. I was born in the middle of that period, and malls were massive at the time of this story. Everyone went there. That kind of rise and fall over time is called a life cycle.

12

I shut up about the watch at school. Just to avoid getting picked on.

But I still wanted it.

It was for sale at only one store in the mall. Every time we went, I'd look at it in the case there.

One clerk at that store (call him Casey) saw my interest. "Christmas is coming!" he kept saying.

My parents knew I wanted the watch but made no promise. Or maybe Santa Claus would bring it for me? Let's just say I had my doubts about that.

I worried as I saw the watches get sold and leave the case, because Casey said no more were coming.

As Christmas approached, there were only two left. Then one. Then none.

This story includes a present that I loved, but it's important to remember that many great gifts aren't things you can hold. A smile is a gift. Saying thank you is a gift. Sunrises, sunsets and stars are gifts. There are no greater gifts than family and friends. Many scientific studies show that gratitude helps you stay strong and positive. Life always includes negatives and losses, but the more you look for gifts, the more you will find them.

13

Christmas came ... and one of my presents from my parents was that watch! I put it on and could hardly wait to show my friends.

But that night I realized that Smash would pick on me about it at school. I fell asleep happy about Christmas but torn about my watch.

THE SPANIARD with his daughter Gracie

(also see page 71)

What is your relationship with your parents or other caregivers? Is it only that you have to do what they say? I hope that, most or much of the time, you find that you want to do what your parents want because of what they do for you. If your home life is a struggle, I'm very sorry. My wish for every kid is for them to be surrounded by love and care, including adults they find easy to respect. If your family life is hard, please talk with your teachers, counselors and coaches at school.

14

I did take my watch to school the day after Christmas, but I kept looking out for Smash. Whenever I thought there was any chance I would see him, I took off my watch and hid it in my pocket.

Then suddenly, there he was. And get this: Smash now had the same watch!

I had hidden my watch away, so he didn't know I had it. "See?" he said, "Too much watch for you, but not for me!"

It was humiliating. It especially bothered me that my parents had spent money on a gift that I wanted but was too afraid to wear.

But I kept hiding it.

After a couple weeks, I got another surprise.

Don't trust rumors, because they often twist as they spread. Have you ever played the game "Telephone"? Everyone lines up, and the person on the end whispers a few words that only the next person can hear, and that person whispers the same words to the next person, and so on. The person at the end announces the words, and almost always, they are radically or even ridiculously changed. That's because we miss details in what we hear and unknowingly change those details slightly in the telling, even when we try hard not to. That's how it is with rumors. A story told and retold often changes until it's completely changed.

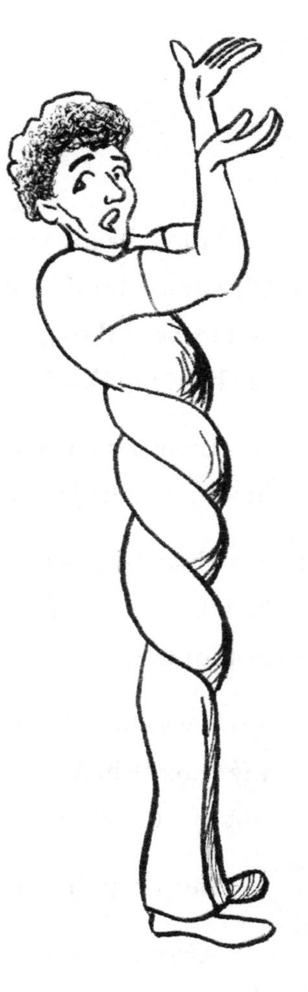

15

About two weeks after Christmas, I was surprised to see that Smash was no longer wearing his watch. He caught me looking at his empty wrist and gave me a sour look. I heard rumors that someone had taken it away from him.

Meanwhile, one place I did feel free to wear my watch was at the mall, because I never saw Smash there. But over the weekend that's exactly where I ran into him. It was too late to hide my watch.

I saw a surprised and angry look come over his face. We both quickly turned and walked away.

That night I was more miserable than ever. Because now Smash knew my secret—that I had the same watch that he used to have. I was disgusted with myself for being afraid to wear my watch.

And now there was a new problem.

At times, any of us might feel like a victim. When things are going wrong, and when enemies seem to be against us. But in this story, look for how I caused some of my own problems. Do you see what I see? What I had done to put myself in a bad place?

16

If I wore the watch now, it would look like I had stolen Smash's watch! It would even look like I was rubbing in the loss of his watch!

Even if that made no sense to anyone. I had never acted anything like a thief, nor had I ever taunted anyone, least of all Smash.

Still, I was certain that Smash would accuse me of both, or one of his gang would. He would push the point and keep after me until he drove me crazy. Even if he didn't believe any of it himself!

I thought more about that last point.

Did you ever feel sorry for the villain in a story? The bad guy? Or someone who treated you badly in real life? Why would that be, when you have great reasons to be angry and bitter at them? With a caring adult, discuss the word EMPATHY.

17

I was sure that Smash knew I hadn't stolen his watch. What flashed on his face at the mall was pain. Whatever the reason, it hurt him not to have his watch. So I truly didn't want to rub in his loss, whether or not he accused me of theft.

Now I was not only miserable but confused.

I was feeling sorry for Smash? After all he had done to me? Why?

I had no idea what to do. All I knew was that this trouble wouldn't melt away on its own. Either I had to do something ... or I would feel forced to do something ... or I would just keep feeling awful.

In the morning when I woke up, I knew just what I was going to do.

Photo by Pascal van de Vendel from Unsplash

A big worry can seem like a thick rope in a huge tangle. But sometimes making one decision can cut through the worst knot like a sharp sword. If you feel knotted up, ask yourself if there is something you need to decide. And something you need to do even if it is hard.

18

I wore my watch to school. I was done dancing around all this. Whatever happened, bring it on.

It played out just as I expected. It started with whispers and pointing at my watch. I heard snippets: "Look at Charlie's watch ... Just like Smash's ... Charlie stole it? ... I thought Smash lost his ... Charlie wouldn't steal it ... Well, it sure looks like he did ..."

Finally, I turned around and found myself facing Smash, and he was pointing at me. His shouts matched the whispers: "You stole my watch! Now you're rubbing it in my face! Deny it, coward!"

"I do deny it," I said. "This is my watch."

"I can prove it's not!" he said.

Whaaat?

There's a great saying: Don't let PERFECT be the enemy of GOOD. Yes, always reach for exactly what you want. Aim high! Be precise! But don't let a fixation on "the best" drive you crazy. Often "falling short" doesn't really matter, and "perfection" doesn't last. This is hard to describe, but watch for a case when "imperfect" gives you all you truly wanted. You'll know it when you see it. I did with my scratched watch.

19

"How can you prove this isn't my watch?" I said, knowing that he couldn't.

"It has a curved scratch on the back," Smash said.

That took me by surprise, and I'm sure that it showed on my face.

My watch *did* have a curved scratch on the back! My parents had explained that to me, saying that Casey had shown them the watch was scratched on the back during handling, but it was the only watch left. They thought that I wouldn't mind the scratch, which I didn't. But how could Smash have known about it?

"Ha!" Smash said, pointing and saying to the crowd. "See! Look at his face! I told you! He stole my watch!"

This might be the very best part of the story to talk about with a caring adult. The key words are: WHO SAYS? If someone says you are a thief, does that make you a thief? If someone besides a parent or other trustworthy adult authority tells you to do something, will you? WHO SAYS who you are and what you will do?

20

“No, I didn’t,” I said. I tried to stay calm. I looked into Smash’s eyes and tried to read his thoughts.

He looked away but finally looked back and growled, “Meet me behind the school at the end of the day and bring the watch.”

“No,” I said.

“No?”

“No.”

I knew what I was going to do instead.

Think of examples of big risks and small risks.
Think of a risk you have taken. Was it big or small?
What made you do it?

21

I took off the watch and reached it out to Smash.

“If you’re so sure this is your watch, take it. But you know it’s not.”

Smash took it, stunned, but finally pulled himself together.

“I still want to see you behind the school later!” he said.

“Fine,” I said. And I walked away.

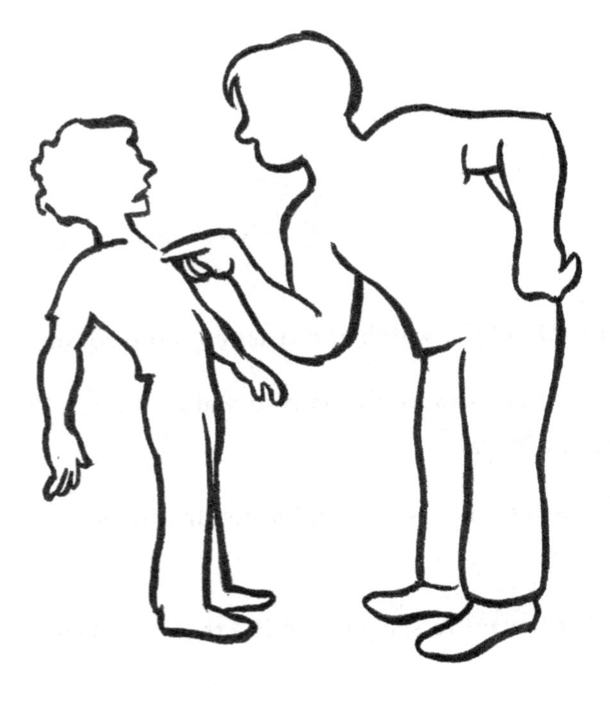

CONFRONTATION is a long word for facing something difficult. Even a child scared of the dark confronts a fear. It's good to be ready to meet hard things head on. I actually "keep in shape" for it by choosing daily discomforts such as cold water plunges, hot sauna sessions, intense exercise and not putting off difficult phone calls. This helps! Watch for small ways to train yourself for bigger confrontations.

22

I missed the watch, but it was different from the misery I had been feeling. I was worried that I wouldn't see it again, especially because it had been a gift from my parents.

At the same time, something told me I had done the right thing. Or *maybe* I had ...

Word got around that Smash and I would meet after school. When the time came, I went behind the building. There was a huge crowd. I made my way into the center.

A ripple ran through everyone. Smash came through everyone and stood in front of me.

I just looked at him.

I noticed he wasn't wearing my watch.

Finally, he made his move.

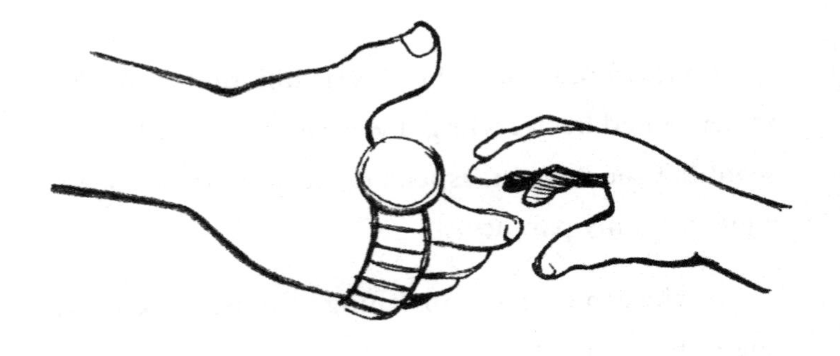

Many wise people, including Abraham Lincoln, said something like this: "I destroy enemies if I turn them into friends." It's hard to do! Some enemies just won't ever be friendly even if you are friendly first. But it's worth trying.

23

Smash reached into his pocket and came out with my watch. He held it out to me.

"Take it," he said.

A different ripple ran through the crowd.

"I didn't steal it," I said.

"I know," he said. "I looked at the back. There's no scratch."

Somehow I managed not to show my surprise. We both knew that there WAS a scratch on the back of the watch. When I took it from Smash, we were both careful not to let the scratch show.

Now I had to figure out what to do next.

In an intense confrontation (that word again!), your brain triggers temporary superpowers through what are called hormones. Really! They make you faster, stronger and tougher than usual. You breathe deeper, and your muscles coil for "fight or flight"—battling or escaping to survive. Just like our taste for stories, this response comes from our early ancestors, who faced dangers daily. That's why after danger passes, you might find yourself tired and panting. You're coming down from the rush!

24

What to say popped into my mind.

"So this was just some kind of mixup?" I said.

"Well, someone took my watch!" Smash said. He looked all around at the crowd. "And I'll find you. Just wait! I'll find you!"

He pushed his way back out. Kids buzzed, then muttered, then drifted away.

I let out a breath.

Some of my friends milled around me for a while, but I replied to them only numbly. I was floating above it all, my mind spinning.

It was over, but it still wasn't over.

Ever wonder why most stores let you return items that you bought? It's to remove risk! Remember when you thought earlier about big and little risks? When a store offers returns with your money back, you basically can buy with NO risk. The store owners know that the only way for them to stay in business is to sell items that most customers won't return and will keep buying and will encourage others to buy. Easy returns help them sell more.

25

I wrestled hard in practice, pulsing with adrenaline from the fight with Smash that had never happened.

Or maybe I had fought, just not physically. My mind kept whirling about it.

After practice at home, my mom said that she had to go to the mall to return something at a store. I went along, because there was something I wanted to check out.

Friendly workers (like Casey in this story) help bring customers some back. That's why some businesses only hire people who smile and are polite during interviews, and who can tell stories about how they stay friendly even when customers are difficult. Remember that when you apply for a job! Also remember that it's just more fun and better for everyone for all of us to be as friendly as possible.

26

I went to the store that my watch had come from. To my surprise, there was one matching watch in the case. Casey was working that evening and saw me looking at it.

"You got another one in after all?" I said.

"Naw," he said. "It was a return."

I could guess where it came from. Smash never did seem to have that much money. Maybe his father made him take the watch back to the store. Or maybe it was his own choice.

"Let me ask you something," I said to Casey.

"Sure!" he said.

All kinds of accidents can happen to items that a store gets in to sell: A scratch, a dent, a crack, a scuff. Or something like fruit can get a bruise or have a soft spot. Many businesses are used to what is called spoilage—damage here or there, while most of the products are fine. Some damaged products can't be sold, but some are sold at a lower price, when an item just doesn't need to be perfect.

27

"When you only had two watches left to sell, how did the other person decide between them? Just pick one?"

"Noooo," Casey said, with a laugh. "They had me take out both watches so they could look them over carefully, front and back. They saw yours had that scratch and took the other. I love what your parents did with that scratch, though."

"Me too," I said.

I have one more well-known saying for you:
Sometimes you can turn lemons into lemonade.
That means something bad can sometimes become something good. Lemons are sour, but by adding sugar they can be turned into a wonderful drink. And guess what? If you come across bruised lemons at a reduced price, that's even better for making lemonade!

28

That night, I sat looking at the back of my watch, trying to see it through Smash's eyes. There was the scratch in the middle, curved just like Smash had said. In fact, it was a long curve, facing up like the letter "U". My parents had it inscribed so it ended up like this, with the scratch acting as a letter "U":

♡ U 4ever
- Mom & Dad

After all this happened, I wore the watch every day until it stopped keeping time and the band ripped. Then I put it in a box for safekeeping.

Also after that, Smash mostly seemed to avoid me.

I finished telling this story to Nicki and watched her face to see what she thought.

Part of caring for anyone is protecting their privacy. It means letting others decide what to tell others about themselves. Many of us find out hidden things about friends and family. Teachers and other caring adults protect many things that are best to keep hidden. Talk to them if you don't know how and when to do that for others.

29

It was hard to tell what Nicki thought. She swallowed and nodded. I held out my hand for a fist bump and got one.

Señora Cruz showed Nicki out and then came back in.

"And now we'll see what happens," she said.

Señora Cruz was choosing her words carefully, because she and I had agreed on one thing about my talking to Nicki.

She never told me Nicki's part in the bullying, and she had asked Nicki not to tell me one way or the other.

So I hadn't known whether I was talking to the bully or to the person being bullied. I still don't.

Let me say a little more about that.

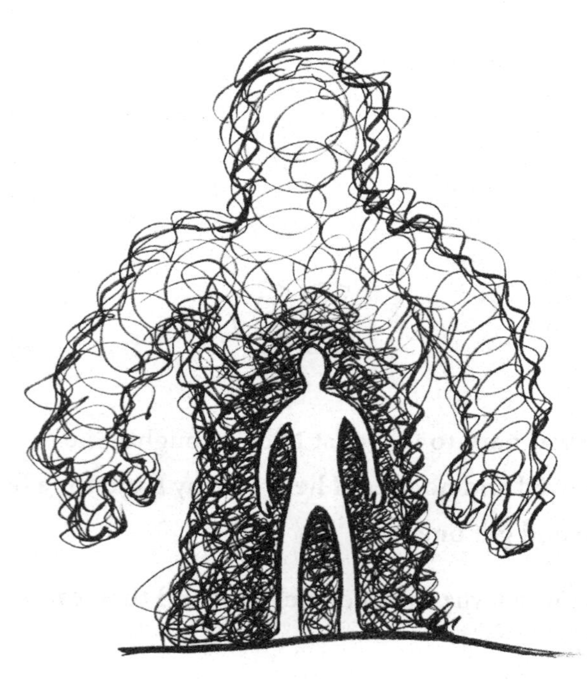

Bullying is terrible. It's cruel. It's painful. It's destructive. It's a terrible thing to face. Sometimes teachers, parents and others who care just can't stop it. My best hope has always been to talk to kids about it directly and help them understand that bullying does come from pain and confusion but that it's always wrong. If you are being bullied or targeted, please keep trying to stay safe and get help. If you see bullying happen, please look for ways to help others stay safe. If you are bullying others, please stop and ask for help. Kindness always wins.

30

Like I said, bullying is sad for everyone. The person being bullied, of course. But also the bully.

Bullies are lonely and fearful. They might not know it, but they're signaling that they need help.

I know that all of this is difficult. I know that it's hard to protect yourself from a bully, much less find a way to help a bully. Sometimes it's impossible.

I know it's hard to find empathy. But it's like what I said about fighting. Being targeted is a test of who you are, who you want to be, and what you can do.

So treat it like every other test. Do your best for yourself, and do your best for others.

I have high hopes for Nicki, whether she has faced bullying or has had to face that she has been a bully. I wish her all good things.

An invitation from

THE SPANIARD

Please watch for the next **DAYS OF SPANIARD** book on Amazon. Teachers and other adults can sign up for updates and free, early access at **charliespaniard.com/days**

I'd love to hear what you
think of the book!
Just leave a review
on Amazon or reach out
on social media
@charliespaniard

Thanks!

- Spaniard

About
THE SPANIARD

Charlie "The Spaniard" Brenneman is a dork with muscles and awesome tattoos. He loves his family, reading, training, and Cinnamon Toast Crunch. A former Division I wrestler, Spanish teacher and UFC fighter, The Spaniard lives in his native Pennsylvania with his wife Amanda and their children Gracie and Rocky. His mission to embody and inspire lifelong learning has led him to podcasting, writing and speaking.

Educational Topics & Discussion Questions

I'm a former teacher. My wife and sister are teachers, and one of my brothers is a principal. I create the DAYS OF SPANIARD series to allow classroom use, including homeschooling. Below are educational topics that this book can help cover with information in the story and related discussions. There are also questions to ask students before and after reading the book so you can measure understanding gained.

- Spaniard

1

Broad topic:	Government and laws
Specific topic:	Respecting the property of others
For discussion:	What does it mean to respect property? Did Charlie and Smash do that?

2

Broad topic:	Communities and citizenship
Specific topic:	How conflicts arise and resolve
For discussion:	What caused the conflict between Charlie and Smash? Was it resolved? If so, how?

3

Broad topic:	Communities and citizenship
Specific topic:	The reason for rules in communities, including schools
For discussion:	The Spaniard competed hard as a wrestler and MMA fighter. How are combat sports different from schoolyard fights? (Emphasize that sport combat happens within rules that help moderate injuries even though risk remains)

4

Broad topic: Continuity and change through history
Specific topic: Changes in women's roles in society
For discussion: What do you think about females competing in combat sports such as wrestling and MMA?

5

Broad topic: Economic interaction
Specific topic: Why goods travel across the nation and world
For discussion: In the story, why did the store in the story run out of the watch that Charlie and Smash both liked? (Reasons not discussed in the story: The watch was probably made far away ... retail stores try to order enough but not in excess ... sometimes demand exceeds supply)

6

Broad topic: Economic interaction
Specific topic: How changes in resources, transportation, communication and technology affect patterns of buying and selling
For discussion: Why do you think the popularity of shopping malls changed over many years? (Reasons not discussed in the story: More malls opened than could serve available customers .... The rise of big box stores, Walmart and other discounters, and online shopping hurt many department stores that anchored malls, as well as chains that leased space in malls ... the rise of video rental and streaming hurt movie theaters located at malls ... many malls came to lack income to use to renovate or innovate to attract new generations)

7

Broad topic: Staying safe and preventing injury

Specific topic: Safety around bullies

For discussion: What are some ways to try to stay safe around bullies? (From the story: Avoid them, ignore them, stay calm, walk away, talk to a bully quietly but firmly, stand your ground, get into a group setting, reach out to an adult. Additional ways: Agree about true differences that a bully picks on and say they don't bother you ... joke with the bully without being insulting)

8

Broad topic: Staying safe and preventing injury

Specific topic: Consequences of unsafe practices such as fistfights

For discussion: What are reasons not to get into fights? (Information not directly shared in the book: Losing personal freedom ... suffering injury ... losing income ... causing harm, distress or inconvenience to others)

9

Broad topic: Staying healthy

Specific topic: Factors that sometimes help cause destructive behavior such as bullying

For discussion: Name things that sometimes lead people to do hurtful things. (From the book: The possibility that Smash's family faces financial stress. Additional things to discuss: Other kinds of stress, influence of peers, body image, social acceptance, influence of mainstream and social media, poor skills in making decisions and refusing actions even if you don't want to do them)

10

Broad topic: Managing home, work and community responsibilities

Specific topic: Avoiding and resolving conflict during communication

For discussion: How does empathy help us get along with others? Can someone have too much empathy?

THE SPANIARD
with his son Rocky

Made in the USA
Middletown, DE
14 October 2023

40693615R00040